SANTA CLAUS is COMIN' TO TOWN!™

Printed in China

9 8 7 6 5 4 3 2
Digit on the right indicates the number of this printing

Library of Congress Control Number: 2007942768

ISBN 978-0-7624-3021-5

Cover and interior design by: Ryan Hayes
Typography: Baskerville MT & Ed-Gothic

Running Press Book Publishers
2300 Chestnut Street
Philadelphia, PA 19103-4371

Visit us on the web!
www.runningpress.com

Santa Claus is Comin' to Town!

Adapted by Sierra Harimann

Illustrated by Mike Koelsch

RP|KIDS
CLASSICS
PHILADELPHIA · LONDON

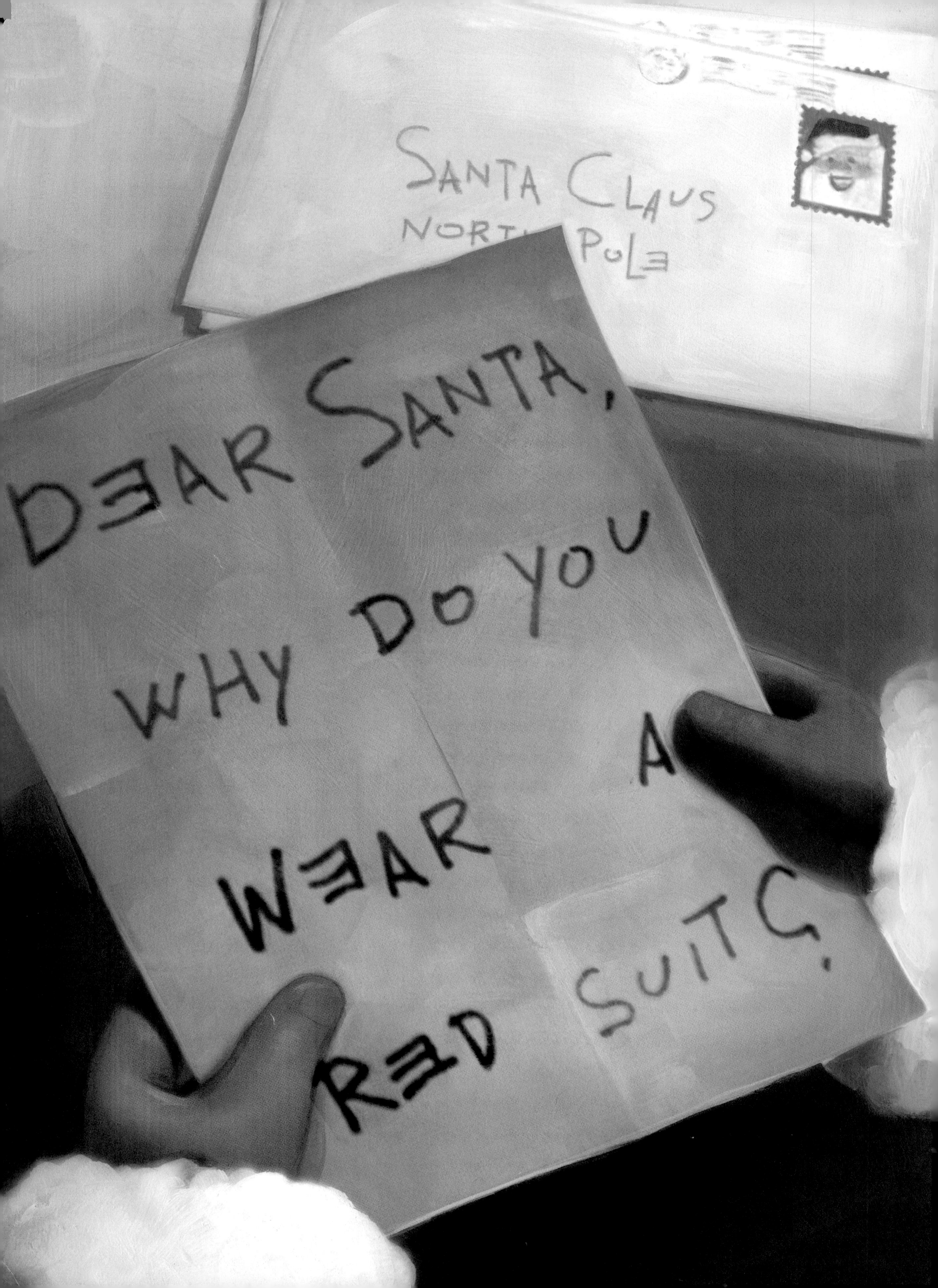
SANTA CLAUS
NORT
POLE
DEAR SANTA,
WHY DO YOU
WEAR A
RED SUIT?

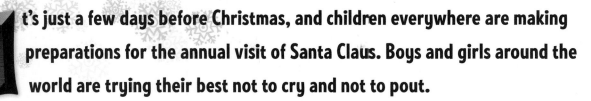

It's just a few days before Christmas, and children everywhere are making preparations for the annual visit of Santa Claus. Boys and girls around the world are trying their best not to cry and not to pout.

Meanwhile, thousands of letters are flooding the postal facilities at the North Pole. And every year the letters for Santa are the same. Some ask for toys, but a lot ask questions. Questions like:

"Why do you wear a red suit?"

"Why do you come down the chimney at night when I'm asleep?"

"Why do you leave presents in stockings?"

"Why is your sleigh pulled by reindeer?"

"Why do some people call you Kris Kringle?"

If you want to know all there is to know about Santa, though, the best place to start is the beginning, when Santa was just a baby. This was years and years ago, in one of the northern countries in a small city called Sombertown. It was a cold, cold place that shivered in the shadows of the strange Mountain of the Whispering Winds.

The people who lived in Sombertown weren't very happy. Their clothes were drab and colorless, and their lives were dreary. The main reason for all this gloom was the mayor—a mean old grouch, who was known as Burgermeister Meisterburger.

One evening, Burgermeister Meisterburger was happily munching on a leg of mutton. Suddenly, one of his soldiers—Grinzley—burst into the room carrying a bundle of blankets.

"Mr. Meisterburger!" Grinzley cried. "Look what was discovered on your front stoop."

"What is it, Grinzley?" Meisterburger barked. "The milk? The daily paper?"

"No, sir," Grinzley replied. "It's a baby!"

Burgermeister chewed a mouthful of mutton, when he began to choke. "A BABY?"

"That's right," Grinzley said. "There's a note. It says, 'Please, sir, take care of my child, and protect him from the dangers of the Mountain of the Whispering Winds. He will be exceptional if only given the love he needs.'"

"Me, take care of a BABY?" he shouted. "Outrageous! What's its name?"

Grinzley held up a small amulet that had been tied around the child's neck.

"This is the only clue," Grinzley said. "It says, 'Claus.'"

Burgermeister shuddered as the baby began to wail loudly. "Take the little—er—baggage—to the orphan asylum. That's the proper place for abandoned children."

"Get the brat out of here!" Burgermeister shouted.

Grinzley didn't argue. He tied the baby to a small sled and headed toward the orphanage, pulling the sled behind him through the bitter cold wind and snow. He trudged along until he glanced back and realized he was pulling a loose rope.

"The sled!" he cried. "It broke away! Where are you, Baby Claus? Come back!"

But it was too late. The wind carried the sled down the road where it hit a bump and veered off into the woods, disappearing behind some trees. The wind continued to blow the sled right up the Mountain of the Whispering Winds and past three deer, who were nibbling on some grass. When the animals saw where the sled was going, they tried to stop it. They knew the mountain was no place for a helpless little baby, for it was the home of the awful Winter Warlock—the strange hermit of the North. He lived alone in a ghostly palace of ice, practicing his strange spells and snowy incantations.

The forest animals knew they had to find a way to hide the baby from the Winter Warlock. So the little rabbits and squirrels covered the baby and sled with branches. They hid the baby just in time, for a few seconds later, the Winter Warlock walked by! But the baby was hidden, and the Winter Warlock moved on.

Relieved, the animals uncovered the baby, and the deer began to pull the sled up the mountain to Rainbow River Valley, a beautiful spot covered with soft white snow. In the valley, right near a bend in the magical stream, there was a tiny cottage with pink smoke coming out of the chimney. It was the home of the Kringles, a jolly family of elves. The animals snuck up to the front door of the cottage very quietly, leaving the baby wrapped in a bundle on the front steps. Then the squirrels and rabbits formed a pyramid until they could reach the doorknocker. They knocked once and quickly scurried away.

The door opened, and an elf named Dingle stepped outside. He had a long, white

"Wiggle my ears
and
Tickle my toes!
methinks I see ∿
∿ a baby's nose!"

beard, and he was dressed in a brightly colored suit trimmed with white fur.

"Yes?" Dingle said. "Who's there? There's who?"

Suddenly, he glanced down at the ground and noticed the small bundle. He did a little dance.

"Ohhh!" he cried. "Wiggle my ears and tickle my toes—methinks me sees a baby's nose!"

He reached down and pulled the blanket aside.

"It's more than a nose," Dingle realized. "There's a whole baby attached to it! Better call me brothers. Wingle! Bingle! Tingle! Zingle!"

Four elves came rushing out of the cottage. They gathered around the baby and scooped him up, passing him from one elf to the next.

"What is it, Dingle?" Zingle asked.

"It's a baby, Zingle," Wingle replied.

"A baby what, Wingle?" Tingle asked.

"A baby baby, Tingle," Bingle said.

"I like babies, Bingle," Dingle chimed in.

"Our baby's the best baby of them all, Wingle!" Bingle said.

The five elves brought the baby inside and handed him to a little old lady elf who was sitting in a rocking chair by the fireplace. She was the elf queen, and her name was Tanta Kringle. She cuddled the baby closely.

"A baby!" Tanta Kringle said happily. "What a splendid idea! He shall live with us, sleep with us, and drink hot cocoa with us!"

"What will we call him, Tanta Kringle?" Zingle asked.

Dingle held up the amulet that had been tied around the baby's neck.

"His license says, 'Claus,'" Dingle told the others.

"That's an unusual name," said Tanta Kringle. "But we shall call him Kris. Kris Kringle!

The Kringles loved baby Kris very much. As he grew older, they set up a little school and taught him all the important things—to read, to write, and to talk.

They also taught Kris how to make toys, because the Kringles were toymakers.

Soon Kris knew how to hammer, carve, and paint a clown made out of wood. The only

problem was that there were no children to receive the toys. All of the boys and girls lived in Sombertown, which was on the other side of the Mountain of the Whispering Winds. The elves couldn't make it past the Winter Warlock to deliver the toys to the neighboring children, so the toys stacked up at the Kringles' factory. Soon there were toys everywhere. One day, Tanta Kringle stood at the window, looking out at the stacks of toys.

"It really is sad," she told Kris. "We'll never be able to get our toys over the mountain."

"Someday, when I'm bigger, I'll take them for you, Tanta Kringle," Kris told her.

"Ahh! That will be wonderful!" Tanta Kringle said happily. "We will be great toymakers again, as we once were."

"When was that, Tanta?" Kris asked.

"Oh, it was years and years ago," Tanta Kringle replied. "The Kringles were known all around the world as the first toymakers to the King."

Right then and there, Kris vowed to make the Kringles' toys famous again someday. As he grew, Kris learned how to make all sorts of beautiful toys. He made toy soldiers, bouncy balls, ballerina dolls, wooden sailboats, fuzzy teddy bears, and shiny trumpets. When he wasn't busy making toys, he was playing outside in the snow with his animal friends. The seals helped teach him how to have fun and how to laugh really hard, like he meant it. Kris could often be heard laughing joyfully, "Ho, ho, ho, ho, ho!"

Years and years passed, and Kris grew into a fine young man. He was sitting with the Kringles around the fireplace one evening when Dingle sighed heavily.

"I am losing my zest for toy-making," Dingle said sadly. "It's all so pointless if no children will ever play with them."

Kris jumped up from his seat. "I'm a man now, Tanta," he said. "I can take those toys across the Mountain of the Whispering Winds."

"It would be nice if someone played with our toys," Wingle said.

"I would be happy if only one of my dollies could be held tightly by a little girl," Tingle agreed.

"It's decided, then!" Kris said happily. "Tomorrow I leave for Sombertown.

Later that night, by the light of the moon, Kris was busy packing a sack full of toys when Tanta Kringle came into the room carrying a large box. "Tanta Kringle!" Kris whispered. "I was just packing. Did I wake you?"

"Oh, no," Tanta Kringle replied. "I was awake anyhow. I made you this for your trip."

She handed Kris the box. He opened it carefully and pulled out a bright red suit that was trimmed with snow-white fur, just like the suits the other Kringles wore. The suit had shiny gold bells on it that jingled when Kris pulled it out of the box.

"Wow!" Kris exclaimed. "It's a real Kringle suit! Thank you, Tanta Kringle."

The next morning, Kris put on his brand-new suit and sadly waved goodbye. He kissed Tanta Kringle on the cheek, slung his sack over his shoulder, and set off down the road.

Just as night was falling, Kris started to make his way through the Dismal Forest, which lay at the foot of the Warlock's mountain. Suddenly, a small black creature leapt out at Kris, causing him to let out a yell and tumble backwards into a snow bank. When Kris sat up and shook the snow out of his ears, he found himself face-to-face with a penguin. The penguin gave him a funny smile.

"Why, you're a penguin!" Kris cried. "What is a penguin doing here?"

The penguin placed his wing against his forehead as though he was searching for something in the distance. Then he pointed to a stick.

"You're looking for a stick?" Kris guessed.

The penguin shook his head.

"A branch?" Kris tried. "A log? A pole?"

The penguin nodded.

"The North Pole?" Kris asked.

The penguin shook his head again.

"The South Pole!" Kris cried. The penguin nodded happily and jumped up and down.

"Well, little fella, that's on the other end of the earth," Kris told his new friend with a chuckle. "You're about as lost as you can get. You'd better travel with me. You need someone to take care of you."

The penguin jumped into Kris's arms and gave him a big kiss on the nose.

Kris put the penguin down. "Come on, er, Topper!" Kris said. "I'll call you Topper, okay?"

Topper made an OK sign with his wing and then honked loudly.

"Ho, ho, ho, ho, ho!" Kris roared with laughter, and the pair continued into the woods.

Suddenly, a terrible voice boomed out from the trees. "WHO NEARS MY MOUNTAIN?"

Kris and Topper froze in their tracks.

"GO BACK OR YOU ARE DOOMED!" the voice called again.

Kris stood up tall. He wasn't going to let the Winter Warlock scare him away so easily.

"Come on, Topper!" Kris called. He and Topper ran as fast as they could over the Mountain of the Whispering Winds. By the time they stopped running, the Winter Warlock was far behind them.

"I'll get him when he returns," the Winter Warlock growled. "He's got to cross my mountain again on the way home!"

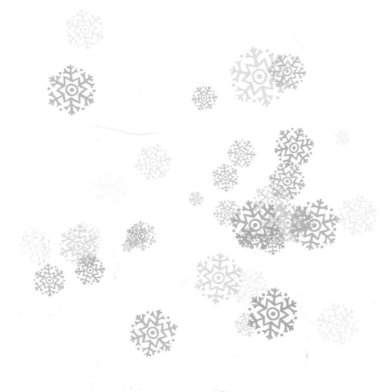

Go back
or you
are
doomed!

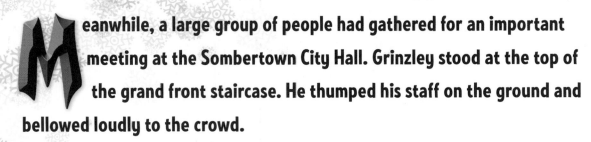

Meanwhile, a large group of people had gathered for an important meeting at the Sombertown City Hall. Grinzley stood at the top of the grand front staircase. He thumped his staff on the ground and bellowed loudly to the crowd.

"Presenting His Honor—Burgermeister Meisterburger!" Grinzley announced.

Burgermeister appeared at the top of the stairway and began his descent. He didn't realize there was a wooden toy duck on wheels sitting on one of the steps. When his foot landed on the duck—whoosh! Burgermeister's feet came out from under him and he bounced head over heels to the very bottom of the steps!

A few hours later, Burgermeister was lying in bed with an ice pack on his head being inspected from head to toe by a doctor.

"Aha!" the doctor cried. "As I suspected. You've broken your funny bone."

"Ohhhh," Burgermeister nodded. "What caused me to trip, Grinzley?"

Grinzley held up the wooden toy duck.

"This, sir!" Grinzley said.

"A TOY!" Burgermeister shouted. "I loathe toys! Toys loathe me! Either they go or I go. And I certainly am not going. Grinzley, I have a job for you."

He leapt out of bed and grabbed a pen and a large piece of paper. He spoke as he wrote,

"Toys are hereby declared illegal, immoral, and unlawful, and anyone found with a toy in his possession shall be placed under arrest and thrown in the dungeon. NO KIDDING!"

Burgermeister handed Grinzley the scroll of paper. "Now post this in the Sombertown Square," he ordered.

Grinzley did as he was told. As the children of Sombertown read the sign, they began to sob.

"We'll never play again," said one little girl sadly.

Just as Grinzley was posting the announcement, there was a commotion at the gates of Sombertown. A man in a bright red suit had just entered the town, followed by a little penguin. It was Kris and Topper!

"Hi, there," Kris greeted people on the street. "Have a nice day, friend."

The townspeople didn't know what to make of Kris. They simply stared at him, or they made rude remarks.

"Don't 'hi' me!" one man grumbled.

"Good morning, ma'am," Kris said kindly to one lady.

"You ought to be ashamed of yourself, young man," she scolded. "You're wearing such outlandish clothes!"

"Clothes?" Kris asked, confused. He stopped in the middle of the town square and turned to face the crowd of people. Then he gestured to the large sack he was carrying. "Look, all I want to do is give away these toys," he told everyone.

The townspeople gasped in horror.

"TOYS?" they shouted. "Eeeeek! Help! Get him out of here! Run! RUN!"

Within a few seconds, everyone in the square had dashed into buildings and houses, shutting the doors and windows behind them. Kris and Topper were left standing in the square alone.

"What did I say?" Kris asked, puzzled. Suddenly, he realized that he and Topper weren't alone in the square—there were a bunch of sad children gathered by the fountain. A girl named Annette and a boy named Andy were busy scrubbing some laundry in the fountain basin.

Kris walked over to the children and put down his heavy sack of toys.

"Well, what's going on here?" Kris asked kindly.

"We're doing our chores," Annette answered.

"Yeah, no more playing," Andy said.

"No playing, eh?" Kris said as he scratched his head, puzzled. "Are you washing out your stockings?"

"Uh-huh," Andy replied. "It's one of our daily duties."

"Then we hang them by the fireplace so they dry overnight," Annette said softly.

"That's the only way they judge you around here." Andy sighed. "They look at how many chores you do and at how clean your stockings are."

"Is that so?" Kris asked.

Andy nodded.

"Well, you don't have to look so glum about it," Kris said cheerily.

"Why not?" Andy said.

"I just don't like sour faces," Kris said. "Now, I've got some real nice goodies for you, but not if you're going to look like this." Kris wrinkled up his nose and eyebrows, making an angry face.

All the children giggled.

"Oh, you'd better watch out," Kris said. "You'd better not cry. You'd better not pout, I'm telling you why."

"WHY?" the children yelled.

"Because I came to town!" Kris said. "And look what I brought!"

He turned his sack upside down, and toys spilled out all over the cobblestone street.

"Toys!" the children yelled.

"Real toys," Andy said.

"Why, sure!" Kris said. "Compliments of the Kringles."

"But what about the Burgermeister?" Annette asked. She was trembling with fear.

"What about him?" Kris replied. "If he wants a toy, he may have one. I'll save him a big red yo-yo!"

Andy and Annette laughed with delight.

"Come on!" they shouted to the other children. "Let's play!"

"WAIT!" A voice silenced the crowd. A young woman with bright red hair tied back in a bun approached the square.

"You must not play with toys," she scolded the children.

Kris walked over to her. "And who are you?" he asked.

"That's Miss Jessica, our new schoolteacher," Annette told him.

"Kris Kringle, at your service," Kris said to Jessica as he bowed deeply.

"How dare you come here in those ridiculous clothes and make fun of me!" Jessica gasped.

"I wasn't making—" Kris began, but Jessica cut him off.

"And what do you mean by giving the children toys?" she asked. "Don't you know toys are against the law?"

Kris did a double take. He couldn't believe his ears! Toys against the law! It was preposterous.

"Really?" Kris asked.

"Yes, it's true," Annette said sadly.

"Well, that's a pretty silly law," Kris said.

"If Burgermeister saw you, we would all be in great danger!" Jessica said.

"In danger from toys?" Kris asked. "Why, that's the silliest thing I've ever heard!"

"Toys are frivolous, impractical, and unproductive," Jessica said coldly. Suddenly, something caught her eye. "Wh—what's that?"

Kris handed her an exquisite china doll.

"For you," he said simply.

"A china doll!" Jessica said as her face lit up with a smile. "I always wanted one when I was a little girl, but my parents would never—oh, thank you!"

"Watch out for that dolly," Kris said with a wink. "She's a hardened criminal, I hear."

Jessica blushed. "Well, maybe it is a silly law," she admitted.

"What do you say you help me hand out these presents?" Kris asked. "It's too big a job for one oversized Kringle and a little lost penguin."

Jessica smiled. "I would be happy to help."

And with that, she and Kris distributed the toys to all of the boys and girls in Sombertown.

"Well, maybe it is a silly law"

The next day in Sombertown was gray and dreary. A group of Sombertown guardsmen accompanied the Burgermeister as he patrolled the town square in his wheelchair, which Grinzley was pushing.

"Ah, a perfect day," Burgermeister said. "Everyone's glum. Ahhh, see the little children playing with their toys."

He sighed happily. Suddenly he realized what he had just said.

"Playing with their toys!" Burgermeister shouted. "Stop! In the name of the law!"

He wheeled himself up to some of the children.

"You brats are under arrest," he barked. Then he turned to the guardsmen.

Kris stepped in front of the children. "Don't arrest those children," he said. "It was my fault. I gave them the toys."

"You?" Burgermeister gasped. "How DARE you? You are obviously a rebel!"

"Me? A rebel?" Kris said with a chuckle.

"Arrest this man immediately!" Burgermeister said.

Kris smiled innocently, and then pulled something from his sack. He handed Burgermeister a bright red yo-yo.

"For you," Kris said.

"What? A yo-yo?" Burgermeister asked, surprised. "I love yo-yos! I used to be able to do all the tricks."

He took the yo-yo and began to bob it up and down.

"Wheeee!" Burgermeister said happily.

Grinzley leaned over and whispered in Burgermeister's ear. "You're breaking your own laws, sir."

Burgermeister suddenly stopped the yo-yo. "I've been bamboozled!" he cried, pointing at Kris. "Arrest him! ARREST HIM!"

The guardsmen charged after Kris and Topper. Kris leapt up and grabbed the branch of a tree. Then he pulled himself up and climbed the tree, with Topper hanging onto his shoulder all the while.

"Egad!" Burgermeister shouted. "He climbs like a squirrel, leaps like a deer, and is as slippery as a seal! AFTER HIM!"

Kris and Topper ran down the road with the guardsmen close behind them, but they were able to escape into the woods.

"Guess we lost them, Topper," Kris said. "Slow down, now. I wonder where we are."

Topper shuddered and pointed to a poster nailed to a tree. It read, "You are trespassing on the lands of the Winter Warlock!"

Suddenly, the trees around Topper and Kris seemed to come to life. There was a terrible roaring sound and the tree branches reached out like gnarled arms, grabbing Topper and Kris and pinning them against two tree trunks.

"Hey!" Kris cried. "Let go!"

A brilliant explosion shook the woods. In a flash of blinding white light, the Winter Warlock appeared in front of Kris and Topper. He laughed an ice-cold laugh.

"Kris Kringle, you've disturbed me for the very last time!" the Winter Warlock said. "Now I have you, and you'll never get away!"

Kris struggled, trying to free himself from the branches.

"Look, before you do me in, would you tell your tree friends to let me loose for a second?" Kris asked politely. "I have something for you."

"What is this, a trick?" snarled the Winter Warlock.

"Oh, no sir, Mr. Warlock," Kris replied. "Or may I call you Winter?"

"Mister Warlock, if you please," the Winter Warlock said sharply.

"Well, I managed to save one little toy, and I'd like you to have it," Kris said.

The Winter Warlock couldn't believe what he was hearing. His angry face sagged, and he looked quite sad.

"You wish to give me a present?" he asked Kris. "A toy?"

"Yes, sir," Kris replied.

"But nobody ever gives mean old Warlock a toy."

"I'd like to start a new custom," Kris said. "Now, if you'd just call off the trees—"

"Of course, of course," the Warlock said with a giggle. "You mustn't mind the tree monsters. Their bark is worse than their bite. Willy Willow, Peter Pine, release the Kringle."

The trees released their grip, and Kris and Topper tumbled into the snow. Kris stood up and brushed himself off.

"No tricks now," the Warlock warned.

"Of course not, Mr. Warlock," Kris replied. Then he reached inside his jacket and brought out a brightly painted toy train. He presented it to the Warlock.

"A choo-choo!" the Warlock cried. "I've always wanted one!"

Suddenly there was a strange gurgling noise, followed by a loud drip that sounded like noisy plumbing.

"What was that?" Kris asked.

"It's my icy heart," the Warlock replied. "It's melting."

"Well, look, Mr. Warlock," Kris began.

"Please, call me Winter," the Warlock interrupted.

"Winter?" Kris asked, surprised.

"Oh, yes," Winter said as he held up the toy train. "Suddenly my whole outlook has changed from bad to good!"

"That's great!" Kris replied. Topper nodded.

"Oh, but will it last?" Winter asked mournfully. "I really am a mean and despicable creature at heart, you know. And it's so difficult to really change."

"Difficult?" Kris said with a laugh. "Why, changing from bad to good is as easy as taking your first step."

"I suppose you're right," said Winter. "There are all kinds of ways we can help each other out. You can bring me nice new toys, and I can help you with my magic."

"How?" Kris asked.

"I'll show you," said Winter as he reached down and scooped up a handful of snow. He packed it into a large, round snowball. Then he held it up in front of Kris.

"Gaze into my magic crystal snowball," Winter told him. "Someone is looking for you."

Kris peered into the crystal snowball and saw Jessica wandering through the woods, calling out his name.

"Jessica!" Kris cried.

"Go to her, lad," Winter said kindly.

Kris took off through the woods, climbing trees to get a better look. When he finally spotted Jessica, he jumped down beside her in the snow.

"Oh!" Jessica cried out.

"It's only me, ma'am," Kris said politely.

"I thought I'd never find you again," Jessica told him. "I wanted to bring you these."

She reached beneath her cape and pulled out a large packet of letters.

"Here are letters and notes from the children of Sombertown," she said. "They're asking for more toys. You see, the Burgermeister destroyed the ones you brought."

"You tell those children they'll have plenty of toys," Kris said. "But only if they behave themselves. No crying and no pouting, or I'll know. Oh, I've got ways of knowing."

He reached down and made a magical snowball out of a handful of snow.

"My personal friend the Warlock taught me this," Kris said. "I can see them when they're sleeping. And I know when they're awake."

"My goodness, you know if they're bad or good?" Jessica asked with a laugh.

"Uh-huh," Kris replied. "So you tell them to be good for goodness sake!"

Kris and Jessica both laughed.

"Oh, thank you, Kris," Jessica said warmly.

"For what?" Kris asked.

"For being so kind," she replied. "For just being you."

She leaned over and kissed him on the cheek.

"Golly!" Kris said as he blushed bright red to match his suit. "Now about the toys—I'll have to slip them in after dark, when the Burgermeister is asleep. So you tell all the boys and girls to leave their doors unlocked tomorrow night."

So Jessica returned to Sombertown to tell the children, and Kris went back to the

Oh, thank you, Kris...
For being so kind.
For just being you.

Kringles to get some more toys.

When the Kringles heard what had happened, they decided to move their toy-making operation closer to the children. So, they moved in with the Winter Warlock, setting up a quaint little toy-making camp.

Meanwhile, Kris made a list of all the children in Sombertown and the toys they wanted. He checked it over once, then he checked it over twice. He tried to figure out who had been naughty and who had been nice.

"Well, I guess they're all pretty nice," he decided. Then he picked up his sack of toys and started off for Sombertown, with Topper right behind him. When Kris was safely inside Sombertown, he tried to open all the doors. If they were unlocked, he knew a child lived inside and was expecting a toy.

The next morning, Burgermeister and Grinzley stood in the center of the town square while the children around them played with toys.

"This is outrageous!" Burgermeister shouted. "There are toys everywhere! What sort of criminal is this Kringle? Sneaking into houses by night? I hereby declare that all the town's doors and windows be locked tight against the prowler."

Despite the Burgermeister's warnings, more and more letters came to Kris from the children. Jessica gathered the letters and gave them to the animals, who delivered them to the Kringles' toy-making camp.

The next time Kris returned to Sombertown with a sack full of toys, he found that all the doors were locked. He had to figure out how to get inside the houses, especially because he had one very special toy to deliver. Suzie, a tiny girl who was very sick, had asked Kris for a toy Noah's ark, and he just had to deliver it to her.

Kris stood in front of Suzie's house, trying to think of a way to get inside. He scratched his head, puzzled. He couldn't disappoint her.

Suddenly, Topper started flapping his wings, honking loudly, and dancing in little circles.

"Shhh!" Kris whispered. "What is it, Topper? You have an idea?"

Topper nodded his head and jumped up and down in the snow. Then he pantomimed opening a door and going inside.

"You have an idea about how to get into the house?" Kris guessed.

Topper nodded again, then waved his wing in front of him to erase the imaginary door. Then he shook his head.

"We won't go through the door," Kris said.

Topper nodded again. Then he pointed up. Kris looked above him at the rooftops of the houses, and finally he saw what Topper meant.

"The chimney?" Kris asked. "You want to go down the chimney?"

Topper danced around in a little circle, delighted and happy. Then he leapt up, kissed Kris on the cheek, and jumped down again.

"Great idea!" Kris exclaimed. He jumped onto a rain barrel and pulled himself onto the roof. He tiptoed across the roof and climbed up the chimney.

"Well, here goes," Kris said. Swoosh! He slid down the chimney. A few minutes later, he popped out of the chimney again, brushing soot off his bright red suit.

"That's fun!" he said with a laugh. "What a great job I've got. Come on, Topper. There are a lot more chimneys to explore tonight!"

The next day, Burgermeister stormed around the town hall, seething with anger.

"More toys!" he shouted. "Discovered by the hearths and mantelpieces! Each house in Sombertown will be searched before dawn. If any more toys are found by the fireplace, they will be confiscated and the children will be severely punished. So be it!"

But the children's letters kept right on coming. The animals delivered a new stack every day. Kris knew he had to figure out another way to get the toys to the children.

Those children must have toys, Kris thought to himself. Otherwise their lives will be nothing but school and chores and washing their stockings and—

His face lit up. "The stockings!" he shouted out loud.

Kris scribbled a note on a slip of paper. He handed it to a robin that was perched on a tree just outside his window.

"Take this to Jessica," he told the bird. "She'll know what to tell the children."

It was another gloomy morning in Sombertown. Grinzley, the Burgermeister, and two guardsmen knocked on the door of one of the houses. A sleepy man in a nightcap answered the door. A woman and two children stood behind him, looking frightened.

"Search the premises!" Burgermeister shouted. "If you find so much as one marble or a half a jack, everyone in the house is under arrest. Double time!"

Grinzley and the two guardsmen searched everywhere. They looked in cupboards, under beds, and inside drawers. Finally, they gave up.

"We can find nothing, Sir Burgermeister," the men reported.

"Good! Very good!" Burgermeister said. "No toys. Nothing but drying stockings, as is proper." He gestured toward the gray stockings that were hanging over the fireplace.

"About face! Forward march!" Burgermeister ordered his men, and they turned to leave.

"Thanks goodness there were no toys!" the father said once the men had left. The children rushed over to the fireplace and tore down the stockings. Then they turned them upside down. Toys fell all over the floor! The children laughed with delight.

Later that afternoon, Burgermeister was walking through the town square when he stopped in his tracks. Children everywhere were playing with toys!

"More toys?" Burgermeister exclaimed. "But how? I will do what I should have done long ago. I will set a trap for that bothersome Kringle. His next visit to Sombertown will be his last!"

Meanwhile, high above the town square, Jessica stood at her window.

"Oh, no!" she cried. "I must warn Kris."

Jessica hurried into the woods and up to the Kringles' camp, but she was too late. Kris had already left for Sombertown with all of his toys. The Winter Warlock stood nearby looking glum.

"Oh, Mr. Warlock," Jessica pleaded. "Winter, please—you must help me stop Kris. Please, use your magic."

Tears rolled down the Winter Warlock's cheeks. "I'm afraid I can't," he told Jessica. "I've

been disenchanted. I have no more powers."

"That's terrible!" Jessica gasped. "What shall we do?"

Suddenly a voice boomed out. It was Grinzley.

"Nobody is going to do anything!" he shouted. He strode into the camp, followed by several guardsmen with drawn swords. The Kringles all leapt to their feet, their hands in the air.

"You're all under arrest for defying the law and making toys!" Grinzley ordered. "And for being an accomplice to Public Enemy Number One—KRIS KRINGLE!"

As the guardsmen prodded them along , the Kringles and the Winter Warlock marched single file though the woods with their hands above their heads. Meanwhile, back in Sombertown, Kris slid down the chimney of his first house. He began filling the stockings with toys. Suddenly, the Burgermeister and two guardsmen leapt out of the shadows.

"Stop!" Burgermeister cried. "You're under arrest."

"Not me!" Kris cried as he turned to escape up the chimney.

"Wait!" Burgermeister pointed out the window. "Look!"

Two more guardsmen held a struggling Topper.

Kris sighed sadly. "What can I do?" he said, holding out his hands to the Burgermeister. "You have me."

"To the dungeon!" Burgermeister cried triumphantly.

The next day, Burgermeister held a victory parade and a bonfire . He piled all of the toys in the center of the town square and lit them on fire. Then he turned to face all the children who had gathered there.

"Children of Sombertown," he addressed them. "You will never, never play again!"

The children cried bitterly. It looked as though Kris had finally been beaten.

As Burgermeister paraded around the square, Jessica rushed over to him.

"Mr. Burgermeister, please," she pleaded. "You must set Kris and the little Kringles free."

"Set them free?" Burgermeister asked with a scowl. "Never!"

"I promise they will never disturb you again," Jessica assured him.

"Bah!" Burgermeister replied. "What good are your promises? Goodbye, good luck, and good riddance!" He exclaimed and marched off.

"My own town, turned against me!" she said sadly. "Well, my eyes are beginning to open for the very first time to what life is really all about with Kris, wherever he is. Today is not the end—it's only the beginning!"

Jessica realized that it was up to her to set Kris and the others free. So she snuck into the dungeon and headed toward the only barred window she could reach. The Winter Warlock came over to the window.

"Mr. Warlock," Jessica whispered.

"Jessica?" the Warlock asked. "Please, call me Winter. What are you doing here?"

"I'm trying to set you all free," Jessica replied. "But I don't know how to do it. Oh, if only you had your magical powers back!"

"Alas, I have nothing but a few meager magical leftovers here in my pockets," Winter said sadly. He opened his robe to reveal many small pockets inside. He removed a few items and placed them on the stone floor.

"A short-circuited wand—useless," he said. "A dried-up magical potion—powerless. The tiny stubs of a hundred or so magic candles—worthless. And just a few handfuls of magic feed corn. It's all junk."

He began putting everything back in his pockets.

"If reindeer eat this feed corn, then they can fly."

"Magic feed corn?" Jessica asked.

"It's of no use to us," Winter said. "It can't dissolve prison walls. All it can do is make reindeer fly."

"Reindeer can fly?" Jessica asked in disbelief.

"Ridiculous, isn't it?" Winter replied. "If reindeer eat this feed corn, they can fly."

"Oh, Winter!" Jessica exclaimed. "That's just what we need! Quick—let me have that corn!"

The Warlock wasn't sure what Jessica intended to do, but he passed her the feed corn anyway. Later that night, Jessica rounded up some of Kris's reindeer friends. She fed each of them a few nibbles of corn, and suddenly, the reindeer lifted off the ground and began to fly!

"Fly!" Jessica called out to them. "On Dasher and Dancer and Prancer and Vixen. And Comet and Cupid and Donner and Blitzen!"

Just around midnight, when the moon was high and bright, those flying reindeer paid a visit to the Sombertown Dungeon. The Dungeon had four walls and was built like a fort, with a courtyard in the center. Burgermeister watched from his window as the reindeer landed in the center.

"Halt!" he shouted. "Stop! STOP!"

Suddenly, one of the reindeer flew out of the courtyard with Kris riding happily on its back.

"Let's go, Donner!" Kris shouted. "Let's go!"

Another four reindeer followed, carrying the Kringles. Then a fifth reindeer flew up, with Tanta Kringle riding regally on its back like a queen.

"Onward, Vixen, onward!" Tanta cried.

Finally, the last two reindeer flew out of the dungeon. One carried the Winter Warlock and the other carried Topper the penguin.

"I still have a little magic!" Winter shouted happily as Topper leapt up and down, honking with delight.

The Burgermeister was very angry.

"We Meisterburgers shall hunt them down throughout the land," he vowed. "Those rebels will not have one moment's peace until they are captured again!"

**K**ris, Jessica, Winter, Topper, and the Kringles fled to the Kringle cottage, but they found it in ruins. "It's not safe here," Kris said sadly. "The guardsmen will be coming back. We'll have to push on."

Jessica moved closer to him, took his arm, and said, "I'll go anywhere you say, Kris".

And so Kris and the others made their way through the woods trying to stay ahead of the Burgermeister and his guardsmen. There were posters tacked all around the woods that read, "Wanted: dead or alive. The terrible toymaker—Kris Kringle!"

But the image of Kris on the poster showed the old Kris. He chuckled as he and Jessica came across one of them in the woods.

"Well, those posters aren't going to do them any good now," he said with a laugh as he stroked the large orange beard he had grown. Still, even with Kris's new look, he was at risk of being caught.

"You should not use your Kringle name," Tanta told him. "It's too dangerous."

"Not call myself Kringle?" Kris asked. "What other name would suit me?"

"There is one," Tanta replied as she removed an amulet from around her neck. "You were wearing this when we found you as a baby. See what it says."

"It says, 'Claus,'" Kris said.

"It's your real name," Tanta said with a sigh. "You must use it now."

So that's how Kris Kringle became known as Mr. Claus. And that's the name he asked Jessica to share when he asked her to be his wife. The two were married in a lovely ceremony on Christmas Eve in the woods. All of the little animals put decorations and candles on the pine trees, and Jessica and Kris put their wedding gifts to each other under the trees.

The Winter Warlock closed his eyes tight, as if to make a wish.

"Oh, please let me have just a little magic left," he whispered. Then he opened his eyes hopefully, took a deep breath, and made a gesture. The candles the animals had placed on the pine trees all lit up at once. It was the very first Christmas celebration.

But soon after the wedding, the group still hadn't found a permanent place to live. They were forced to trudge through the snowy woods, beyond the reaches of civilization. They headed far past the most northern city—past where even most animals lived. They went all the way to the North Pole.

"This is it," Kris said with a sigh. "This is where we'll build ourselves a nice house. While we're at it, we'll build ourselves a castle! And we'll build the best toy factory in the world!"

In no time at all, they built a castle and workshop, and they settled in and started making toys. And they needed toys, because despite everything Meisterburger tried, the legend of Mr. Claus had spread. The animals continued to deliver letters by the thousands.

"Just look at this list!" Kris exclaimed as he unrolled a piece of paper that was eight feet long. "It's taken almost a year to check it once, not to mention twice!"

Jessica laughed.

"Well, it's time to load up the sleigh," Kris continued. "This is the fourth trip this month!"

Because he was still an outlaw, Kris traveled at night. And since he had to get all over the world and back before daybreak, he had built himself a great big sleigh. It was the fastest one in the whole world!

But as time passed, the Meisterburgers died off and fell out of power. And the good people of Sombertown and other cities around the world realized how silly the Meisterburger laws were. Everyone had a great big wonderful laugh, and they promptly forgot all about those silly laws! And the older Mr. Claus got, the more famous he became, and the more folks grew to love him. Soon they were calling him Santa Claus because he was such a good man that people considered him to be just like a saint.

As good as he was, though, Santa Claus could hardly keep up with the toy orders.

"I'm afraid I'm going to have to limit my journeys to once a year," he told Mrs. Claus one night. "But on which night should I go?"

It wasn't a hard decision to make. They chose the holiest night of the year—the night they had celebrated their love for one another. It was Christmas Eve, the perfect night for giving.

And even today, Santa can still look into his magic snowball to see just what all the little boys and girls around the world are up to. And now that you know all about him, you can be sure that no matter what, every Christmas Eve, Santa Claus will be coming to town!